IN AFRICA

By Sandra Beris
Illustrated by David Gantz

A GOLDEN BOOK • NEW YORK
Western Publishing Company, Inc., Racine, Wisconsin

"Wowzers!" said Inspector Gadget. "Africa certainly is exciting, isn't it, Penny?"

"It sure is, Uncle Gadget," said Penny. "And our train ride through the jungle should be the most exciting part."

Inspector Gadget and his niece Penny and their dog Brain were waiting in the station for the Mombasa Express.

"There's a lot to see, even here in the station," said
Inspector Gadget. "Look at that lion hunter!"

"That's no lion hunter," Penny whispered. "I think that's
Chief Quimby, your boss."

And so it was. Chief Quimby had a secret message for Inspector Gadget. It said:

M.A.D. agents want to hijack this train.
Your mission is to stop them.
This message will self-destruct.

"Got it, Chief," said Inspector Gadget.

He dropped the message out the window as the train began to *chug-chug-chug* out of the station. The train pulled out so fast that Inspector Gadget didn't see where the message fell.

KA-BOOM! The message self-destructed right on Chief Quimby's head.

"Why don't I get a new secret agent?" Chief Quimby moaned.

Meanwhile, far away in his dark castle, Dr. Claw was hatching an evil plan. Dr. Claw was the head of *M.A.D.*—which stands for *Mean And Dirty*—and he hated no one more than Inspector Gadget.

Through his video screen, Dr. Claw told his agent on the train just what to do. "Make sure you get that train," he said. "But most of all, get Gadget!"

"I will, boss," the agent promised.

As the train whizzed through the jungle, Inspector Gadget and Penny and Brain were settling into their cozy compartment. The porter showed them around their little room.

"The beds open up like this," he said. "They're very comfortable. Why don't you try one?"

"I could use a nap," Inspector Gadget said with a yawn. He climbed into one of the beds.

SWACK! The bed crashed shut with Inspector Gadget in it.

"Go, go, Gadget coat!" said Inspector Gadget.

His coat blew up bigger... and bigger...until the bed popped open.

"They don't call me 'Gadget' for nothing," Inspector Gadget said proudly.

"Curses!" snarled the porter, and he hurried down the hall.

"No need to let a little accident upset you," Inspector Gadget called after him.

But Penny was not so sure it was an accident. "I think that porter is a *M.A.D.* agent," she told Brain. "It's time for your jungle monkey disguise. Snoop around and see what you can find out."

"R-r-oh r-r-ay!" barked Brain. That was his way of saying "okay."

That evening in the fancy dining car, Inspector Gadget couldn't keep from staring at a nearby table. "What's a monkey doing in here?" he whispered to Penny. "Maybe that's the *M.A.D.* agent Chief Quimby warned me about."

Penny secretly winked at Brain. She didn't see the waiter coming toward them with a loaded tray. But then...CRASH! He dropped the tray right on Inspector Gadget's head. Inspector Gadget was knocked out.

"Why, that waiter is the *M.A.D.* agent who slammed the bed on Uncle Gadget!" Penny shouted. "After him, Brain!"

Brain chased the waiter all through the train. When they reached the last car, Brain stopped in surprise. Standing before him was the biggest elephant he had ever seen.

"You won't catch me!" said the waiter. "Dr. Claw sent along this speedy elephant so I could make a quick getaway. And here I go!"

He leaped onto the elephant's back, and the elephant leaped through the side of the car. Brain grabbed its tail just in time.

Back in the dining car, Penny was trying to tell Inspector Gadget what had happened. But he wouldn't listen.

"I have no time for small talk," he said. "Now which way did that strange-looking monkey go?"

Inspector Gadget and Penny made their way through the train. Soon they came to the last car. "So," said Inspector Gadget, "that *M.A.D.* monkey escaped by elephant!"

"But the monkey isn't..." Penny tried to explain again.

"Not now, Penny," said Inspector Gadget. "I'm going after him. Go, go, Gadget copter!" And away he flew.

Brain was still bumping along behind the getaway elephant. At last it stopped. Brain jumped down and hid in the bushes. The agent climbed down and set to work placing sticks of dynamite on the railroad tracks.

Dr. Claw was watching on his video screen. "We couldn't get Gadget on the train," he snickered, "but no matter. We'll simply blow up the whole train—and Gadget with it!"

Inspector Gadget was not getting very far with his copter, but he knew there was not a minute to lose. "That monkey will get away," he cried. "Go, go, Gadget skates!" And away he rolled, down the tracks.

From the train, Penny buzzed Brain on their two-way watches. Through her watch's tiny video screen, Penny was able to see the *M.A.D.* agent lighting the fuse. "Dynamite!" she exclaimed. "Stop him, Brain!"

Brain turned the long tail of his monkey costume into a lasso. He twirled the tail and threw it.

Just then Inspector Gadget came rolling by. "Wowzers!" he shouted as he came crashing down on the agent.

"You should never play with matches," said Inspector Gadget to the agent. "It could be dangerous, especially with all these trees around." He blew out the match and stood up to brush himself off. Brain tied up the agent.

The train was coming around the bend, but it squealed to a stop just in time. Everyone hurried out to see what had happened. Chief Quimby flew in by helicopter.

"Congratulations, Gadget," he said. "You've captured the *M.A.D.* agent!"

"Good work, Brain!" said Penny.

Dr. Claw saw everything on his video screen. "I'll get you next time, Gadget!" he said.

After all the excitement, Inspector Gadget and Penny and Brain were happy to spend a few quiet days at the beach. And a new friend was with them.

"You were right about that train ride, Penny," Inspector Gadget said. "It was the most exciting part of our trip so far."

"Yes," said Penny. "But now I'm looking forward to our nice quiet elephant ride home."